N E LINCS LIBRARIES

5 4073 02019154 2

KT-444-369

DINOSAUR CLUB

Catching th[e ... Raptor]

NORTH EAST LINCOLNSHIRE
LIBRARIES

WITHDRAWN
FROM STOCK

AUTHORISED:

Written by Rex Stone
Illustrated by Louise Forshaw

Jamie has just moved to Ammonite Bay, a stretch of coastline famed for its fossils. Jamie is a member of Dinosaur Club – a network of kids who share dinosaur knowledge, help identify fossils, post new discoveries, and chat about all things prehistoric. Jamie carries his tablet everywhere in case he needs to contact the Club.

Jamie is exploring Ammonite Bay when he meets Tess, another member of Dinosaur Club. Tess takes Jamie to a cave with a strange tunnel and some dinosaur footprints. When they walk along the footprints, the two new friends find themselves back in the time of the dinosaurs!

It's amazing, but dangerous too – and they'll definitely need help from Dinosaur Club…

CONTENTS

CHAPTER 1

Jamie Morgan pulled a rainbow-coloured metal fish out of his grandad's fishing box and held it up for his friend Tess Clay to see. "This fish has feathers!" A cluster of tiny pink and orange feathers sprouted out from where the tail should be.

"Different baits catch different beasts," Jamie's grandad, Commander Morgan, said with a grin. He held out his hand for the feathery fish. "This spinner is great for catching sea bass. Now, let's see. What else will I need today?" He tipped a tangle of weights, spinners and fishing line onto the kitchen floor of the old lighthouse.

"What's this?" Jamie picked up an H-shaped piece of orange plastic with string wrapped around it and a couple of heavy lead weights dangling from it.

"Haven't you seen one before?" Tess said in amazement. "It's a crab line."

Jamie shook his head. "How can this catch crabs?"

"It's easy," Tess said. "You tie a bit of bacon rind on the end and throw it in. The crabs grab the bacon and you grab the crabs!"

"Cool!" said Jamie. "I'd like to try that."

"The best place for crabbing is Sealight Head at high tide," Commander Morgan said, as he crammed everything but the crab line back in his fishing box. "But high tide isn't until later this afternoon. I'll meet you there if you like, after I've caught some sea bass for dinner."

"Okay, Grandad," Jamie said as Commander Morgan finished packing his tackle box. "We'll wait until then."

"We don't have to wait," Tess whispered to Jamie. "We could go crabbing in Misty Lagoon in Dino World right now."

Dino World was Jamie and Tess's biggest secret – even Commander Morgan didn't know that they'd found a way into a world where real live dinosaurs lived.

The only people they'd told were their friends in Dinosaur Club, a group of kids from around the world who loved dinosaurs as much as Tess and Jamie.

"Great idea!" Jamie grinned at Tess. "We'll meet you near Sealight Head later, Grandad."

"Don't forget the bait and mop bucket to put the crabs in," Commander Morgan told them. He pulled on the sturdy boots he wore when he was running the coast guard. "And I've put two cheese and spicy chilli chutney sandwiches in the fridge for you." He headed for the door. "Have fun!"

"We will," Tess said with a smile. The minute the commander was out the door, Tess grabbed the handle of the mop bucket. "Got your tablet, Jamie?"

"Already in my backpack."
Jamie grinned as he wrapped
the sandwiches in cling film
and made a separate package for the
bacon. He stuffed them in his backpack
along with the crab line. "Let's go to
the Cretaceous period!"

The two friends clattered down the
stairs of the lighthouse, and dashed
through the dinosaur exhibits in the
museum on the ground floor. Jamie's
mum was busy fixing a label to the wall
next to the triceratops skull.

"How's the museum going, Dr
Morgan?" Tess asked.

"Great, thanks, Tess," said Jamie's
mum. "The Grand Opening is only a
few days away!"

"See ya, Mum!" Jamie called, hurrying past the Late Cretaceous model and the T. rex display. "We're going crabbing."

Jamie and Tess scrambled down the rocky path from the lighthouse and ran along the beach onto the trail that led up Smuggler's Point. They bent double to catch their breath, and then clambered up the boulders to the smugglers' cave and squeezed through the gap at the back into the secret chamber.

"This is my favourite place in the whole world!" Jamie's heart began to pound as soon as he placed his feet over the fossilised dinosaur footprints on the cave floor.

"One… two… three…" He counted each step. "Keep close behind me, Tess."

"You bet." Tess's voice sounded excited. "I wonder what we're going to find this time."

"Four…" A crack of light appeared in the cave wall in front of them.

"Five!" The ground squelched beneath Jamie's feet and he stood blinking in the bright sunshine and breathing in the familiar warm wet-leaf smell of Dino World.

CHAPTER 2

A second later, Jamie and Tess were standing on Ginkgo Hill, and a scaly nose was rubbing Jamie's hand.

"Ready for another adventure, Wanna?" Jamie asked their little dinosaur friend.

Jamie picked a stinky ginkgo fruit and held it out to the wannanosaurus.

Wanna took it gently, then greedily gobbled it up, wagging his tail and grunking as smelly ginkgo juice dribbled down his chin.

"It's almost like he was waiting for us," Tess said with a laugh.

"Then let's go crabbing! We've only got until the tide comes in."

With Tess and Wanna close behind, Jamie strode through the trees to a curtain of creepers at the edge of Ginkgo Hill. As he pushed the creepers aside, excitement fizzed like lemonade in his stomach.

Beneath them lay the steamy emerald-green jungle. The air throbbed with the whirring and buzzing of insects, and the jungle rang with the strange calls of the weird and wonderful creatures that only lived in Dino World.

"This has got to be the best place for adventures in the whole wide world!"

Jamie announced with a huge grin on his face.

"In the whole solar system!" Tess cheered.

"In the whole universe!" Jamie exclaimed.

Wanna grunked his agreement.

"Come on!" Jamie said. "Let's see what we can catch in Misty Lagoon."

The three friends clambered down the steep hillside into the dense jungle.

"We can follow the stream," Jamie said, jumping into the shallow water that trickled and gurgled its way to the lagoon. They splashed along the stream bed.

"That's where we met the T. rex," Tess said, pointing to a jumble of huge rocks.

"I'll never forget those fangs."
Jamie shuddered. "I hope it's not
around today."

"Me too," said Tess, looking around
nervously. "Let's get a move on."

They ran until they burst out of the
jungle onto the sandy beach of the
sparkling blue lagoon.

Jamie shaded his eyes with his hand and gazed round the shore. "Which would be the best spot to find prehistoric crabs?"

"We need deep water for crabbing," Tess told him. "It's no use wading into the shallows."

"How about over there?" Jamie pointed to an outcrop of fern-covered rocks on the north shore. A stone ledge stuck out of the ferns like a wide diving board, hanging over the deep blue water.

"Perfect!" Tess declared.

Jamie led the way around the lagoon to the rocks and scrambled on top of them, pushing aside the plants. It was an easy climb to the ledge over the water, and he put down his backpack in the shade of the tall ferns.

Tess scrambled up onto the ledge next to him. "We can't see much behind us through these ferns," she said, glancing over her shoulder. "But Wanna will warn us if anything tries to sneak up on us."

She leaned over the lagoon and filled up the bucket with water. "Time to bait the line."

Jamie knelt on the rock ledge, pulled off his backpack and dug inside it.

"Here's the bacon," Jamie handed Tess a clingfilm packet and then unravelled the crab line.

Wanna watched curiously as Tess unwrapped the bacon.

"No, Wanna, it's not for you," Tess told the little dinosaur, tearing off the bacon rind. Wanna leaned over Tess's shoulder, eyeing the bacon greedily.

Gak gak gak! Wanna spluttered in disgust. He spun around and grabbed a mouthful of fern leaves.

"He's trying to get rid of the taste," Jamie said, tying the bacon rind onto the end of the line. "Plant eaters don't eat bacon."

Tess showed Jamie how to hold the orange plastic handle and carefully lower the crab line into the lagoon. Jamie felt the string run through his fingers until the weight came to rest on the bottom.

"Do I pull it up straight away?" he asked.

"No." Tess laughed. "You have to be patient. You'll feel a tug on the line when something takes the bait."

"What if it isn't a crab?" Jamie asked. "What if it's a huge electric eel?"

"Ooh," Tess said. "What if it's a humongous stingray?"

"What if it's a Loch Ness Monster with gigantic fangs?" As Jamie laughed, a big bubble broke the mirror surface of the water.

Pop!

Jamie leapt to his feet, startling Wanna who nearly fell backwards over the bucket. But there was no tug on the line. The lagoon was a mirror once more.

"False alarm," Tess said. "There's nothing there."

Wanna started chewing on the stems.

"Wanna's got the right idea," Jamie said. "Let's have lunch while we wait."

"Good idea," Tess rummaged in the backpack, pulled out a sandwich and handed it to Jamie.

"Your grandad's chutney is great!"
Tess mumbled with her mouth full. "Even
if it is spicy!" she said between coughs.

"It really is," Jamie agreed, taking
a huge bite. He felt a tug on
the crab line.

"Something's taken the
bait!" Jamie spluttered,
spraying a mouthful of crumbs
all over the rock. He threw
down his sandwich and started
to pull up the line as fast as he
could. The line went limp.

Tess and Jamie peered over
the ledge. "It got away," Jamie realized,
as the end of the empty line came out
of the water. "It ate the bacon, too."

"Better luck next time." Tess tore off another strip of bacon and fixed it to the line. Jamie threw it back in the water and reached for his sandwich.

"Where's my sandwich gone?" he said. There was a rustle in the ferns. Jamie whirled around.

"Wanna!" Jamie yelled. "You sandwich thief!"

Jamie gave the handle of the crab line to Tess and hopped off the rock into the ferns. He could hear a strange high pitched rattling noise.

Ack ack ack!

Jamie hadn't heard Wanna make that noise before.

"Wanna?" he called. "Is that you?"

The ferns parted. The little dinosaur

was bobbing his head and hopping excitedly from foot to foot as he made gak-gak noises.

Jamie knew what that meant; Wanna must have been spluttering on Grandad's pickle. "It's your own fault. You shouldn't have stolen my sandwich," Jamie scolded him.

"Come quick!" Tess shouted from behind him. "We've caught something!"

CHAPTER 3

"One, two, three… Heave!"

Jamie and Tess pulled on the crab line with all their might.

"Look at the size of that!" Tess gasped.

Dangling from the crab line was the biggest crab that Jamie had ever seen. Its shell was the size of a dinner plate. The crab's silvery shell shined in the sunshine as it gripped the bacon on the line.

As Tess held the line, Jamie grabbed
the bucket.

Wanna edged up and sniffed at the
crab. It waved a pincer at him.

Grunk!

Wanna jumped back in alarm as Tess lowered the crab gently into the bucket.

"It's a good job this is a big bucket!" Jamie laughed.

They peered into the bucket. The crab was using its pincers to tear off small pieces of the bacon and shovel them into its mouth.

"Crabs haven't changed much since dino times," Tess said thoughtfully.

Jamie took out his tablet. He opened the DinoData app and typed CRAB into the search box. "Crabs haven't changed much since dinosaur times," he read aloud.

Tess laughed. "That's what I said."

Jamie put the tablet on the rock beside him. "I want to take a close look at this crab," he told Tess. "Help me get it off the line. It's wedged in the bucket, so it shouldn't nip us."

Wanna looked over their shoulders as Tess held the bucket steady and Jamie gingerly untangled the line from the crab's pincers.

Just when he had finished, there was a sudden rustle in the ferns behind them.

Ack ack ack!

Jamie spun round to see what was
making the noise. A turkey-sized dinosaur
with open toothy jaws dashed out from
the plants onto the ledge beside them.

Tess almost dropped the bucket
in surprise.

Snap! The new dinosaur grabbed the
tablet in its needle-sharp fangs.

Ack ack ack ack ack!

With a whip of the feathers on the end of its long yellowy-green tail, the dinosaur turned and darted into the ferns.

"What was that?" Tess said, still holding the bucket.

"Th-that…" stammered Jamie, feeling the blood drain from his face. "That was a velociraptor. A velociraptor just stole my tablet!"

"What?" Tess didn't look happy. "They're supposed to be vicious and really fast."

"It's got my tablet," Jamie said, shoving the crab line into his backpack. "We have to get it back."

Jamie crashed into the tall ferns and chased after the rapidly retreating raptor. Tess and Wanna plunged after him.

"It's heading towards Far Away Mountains," Tess panted, as they emerged from the ferns into a section of the plains they hadn't been to before.

"Why did you bring the crab?" Jamie asked as they puffed along a shallow steam that flowed down to the lagoon.

Tess looked down at the bucket that swung from her hand in amazement. "I forgot I had it," she said. "I'll take it back later."

Ahead of them, the velociraptor darted into a narrow passageway where the stream gushed between two huge rocks.

"Careful," Tess said. "The raptor might be lying in wait. We don't know what's on the other side of the rocks."

"Time to find out." Jamie stepped into the cool, fast-moving stream. Edging sideways like a crab, he squeezed through the narrow gap, followed closely by Tess and Wanna.

"Wow," he breathed. "It's like a rainbow!"

Ahead of them, the stream flowed through wide rocky steps streaked with splashes of bright orange, yellow and green, and cratered with deep aquamarine pools that sparkled in the sunshine.

"There's the raptor!" Tess pointed to a feathery tail disappearing into a cave on the other side of the pools.

"That must be where it lives." Jamie heaved a sigh of relief. "Ugh!" he sputtered. "It stinks of rotten eggs around here."

"Wanna likes it," Tess said, glancing at the little dinosaur. Wanna was standing next to one of the small pools, with his snout in the air, sniffing deeply.

"He would," Jamie laughed. "He likes anything stinky."

Wanna cocked his head to one side and peered into the pool.

"Is he looking for more crabs?"

As Tess spoke, Wanna's pool burbled and bubbled. Pop! A whisp of hot steam escaped from a burst bubble and the smell of rotten eggs welled up.

"The water's hot," Jamie chuckled. "The only crabs he'll find in there will be cooked ones."

Suddenly, there was a great whoosh!

Wanna leapt back from the pool as a column of steaming water gushed high into the air.

Jamie watched it, mesmerised.

"Get out of the way!" Tess yelled as the column collapsed and a torrent of scalding water fell towards them.

CHAPTER 4

Jamie, Tess and Wanna dived behind
a rock as scalding drops of water
rained down.

"It's a geyser," Tess said excitedly. "I
saw one on a TV programme about
Yellowstone Park. The water's heated
up by melted rock that bubbles up from
the centre of the Earth where the crust
is thin."

The friends peered out from behind the rock. On the other side of the pools, near the raptor's cave, there was a hissing and popping like a cork and another geyser whooshed and spurted into the air. Each of the six pools took their turn to shoot jets of hot water into the air.

"No wonder that velociraptor's chosen to live in this cave," murmured Tess. "What other dinosaur would be fast enough to run past all the boiling geysers?"

"If we're careful, we can do it," Jamie said. "We've got to get the tablet back. If we leave it behind here, it might get fossilized – then someone in the future could dig up a computer next to a dinosaur fossil. We'll just have to learn the geysers' pattern."

The two friends watched as the geysers repeated their eruptions.

"I think I've got it," Jamie said.

The valley had gone quiet again. The only sound was the stream. It was as if nothing had happened.

"Now!" Tess yelled, clutching the crab bucket to her chest.

Jamie, Tess and Wanna sprinted past the first pool.

Whoosh!

A huge geyser shot into the air behind them.

"Watch out!" Jamie shouted. The three jumped into the stream and hid under an overhanging rock as the hot

rain pattered into the water. As soon as it
had passed, Wanna darted out and
dashed past the second pool and the
third, dodging the bubbling water.

"Follow Wanna!" Jamie yelled to Tess,
and they raced after their dinosaur friend
as all around them steaming fountains of
scalding water exploded from mini-geysers.

In front of the cave, an aquamarine
pool began to gurgle.

"Geyser about to blow!" Tess shouted above the sound of the fast-flowing stream. Jamie, Tess and Wanna sprinted past the gurgling pool and hurled themselves behind a rock at the edge of the cave mouth as the last geyser exploded with a whoosh!

"That was close," Tess panted, and then peered into the bucket. "The crab seems to be okay. It's waving its pincers, though. I think it's annoyed."

"I'm not surprised." Jamie grinned, glancing at his watch. "We have to hurry," he told Tess. "It'll be high tide soon. We've got to get back before Grandad comes looking for us."

"Sshh!" Tess whispered. "Wanna can hear something."

Wanna was peering into the cave, with his tail sticking out stiffly behind him.

Ack ack ack ack ack!

A high-pitched rattle came from the back of the cave. Wanna shot backwards, making grunking noises.

"Hide!" Jamie hissed. They ducked back behind the rock.

"We'll have to be careful," Tess whispered, gently putting down the crab bucket. "That's the raptor's den, and animals are dangerous if you corner them in their den."

They peered into the cave. Against the wall, near the entrance, was a nest like a bird's, but woven of dried ferns, and the size of a car tire. The sun was sparkling on something shiny.

"There's the tablet!" said Tess.

Jamie breathed a sigh of relief. "It's really close and there's no sign of the raptor. He must have gone deeper into the cave. Maybe we can just grab the tablet and get out of here."

Tess nodded. "Let's try."

They quietly crept into the gloomy, dank cave and tiptoed towards the velociraptor's nest. Jamie's foot crunched on something. Ugh! He looked down and shuddered. Well-gnawed bones were scattered around the huge nest.

"It's like the nest of a giant bird of prey," Tess whispered from behind him. "If that raptor gets us, it'll pick our bones clean."

A prickle of fear ran down Jamie's spine. He knew they had to be very careful.

Suddenly, the velociraptor shot out of the darkness, snarling viciously.

Ack ack ack ack ack!

CHAPTER 5

Jamie threw himself backwards as the raptor pounced.

Snap! The raptor's needle-sharp teeth closed on empty air.

"Get out! Quick!" Tess grabbed Jamie by the T-shirt and pulled him out of the cave and back behind the rock, nearly knocking over the dino crab bucket in the process.

Once more, they peered gingerly around the rock.

Ack ack ack ack ack!

The velociraptor was rattling softly to itself as it bent over its nest and nosed at the tablet. The whoosh of the geysers exploded down the valley, drowning out all sound.

"If we lure it out of the cave," Jamie whispered to Tess, "then I can dash in and grab the tablet."

"I've still got some of my sandwich…" Tess said. "But the velociraptor is a carnivore."

Jamie glanced at the crab in the bucket. "I've got an idea!" He rummaged in his backpack, took out the crab line, and tied on the remains of the bacon.

"Cool!" Tess grinned, taking the line. "I've never crabbed for dinosaurs before."

Tess scrambled up onto the rocks above the cave and lowered the crab line so that the bacon dangled at raptor height in the mouth of the cave.

The valley quietened again as Jamie and Wanna flattened themselves behind the rock at the side of the cave entrance. Wanna grunked softly to himself.

"We have to be patient, like we're crabbing," Jamie told the little dinosaur.

Suddenly, the raptor lunged out of the
mouth of the cave reaching for the bacon
with its sharp talons, but Tess jerked the
crab line up and away. The raptor spread
the feathers on its tail and forelimbs and
launched itself into the air after the meat,
but it was too high.

Tess lowered the bacon again to just in front of the vicious dinosaur, but pulled it away before it could grab it. The raptor leapt again and snaped at the bacon on the end of the line.

"It's like a kitten playing with a piece of string," Jamie whispered to Wanna.

Tess edged along the rock shelf above the mouth of the cave, taking the bacon bait farther and farther away from where Jamie and Wanna were hiding.

"It worked!" Jamie said. He darted into the cave and grabbed the tablet out of the nest. He glanced around the nest. There was the film that his sandwich had been wrapped inside – the raptor had stolen his sandwich, not Wanna!

I can't leave that to get fossilized, he thought, snatching it up and stowing it in his backpack with the tablet. Jamie kept to the shadows and crept back the way he had come.

So far, so good, he thought, and he poked his head cautiously out of the cave.

Instead of seeing Wanna's friendly face, two cold reptilian eyes stared unblinkingly back at him.

"Oh no!" Jamie breathed.

The velociraptor was back. It tilted its head to one side.

Ack ack ack!

The raptor rattled ominously and began to twitch its tail from side to side.

Jamie's blood ran cold. It looked like a cat preparing to pounce on its prey.

"It's going to attack!" Tess screamed from the ledge above as the velociraptor spread its talon-like claws and came towards Jamie.

CHAPTER 6

Jamie froze on the spot. Any moment now, the raptor's sharp teeth and claws would tear him to pieces.

Something scratched at the ground behind him. Jamie whirled round. Wanna! Wanna was revving up, getting a claw hold on the rock, his bony head lowered...

Gaaaaak!

The little dinosaur charged just as the velociraptor sprang at Jamie.

Thwack! Wanna barged into the velociraptor and bowled it over.

As the raptor spat and rattled furiously, struggling to get back to its feet, Jamie and Wanna raced to the safety of the rock

"Mind the crab!" Jamie yelled. Too late. Wanna's tail smacked into the bucket and knocked it over. Jamie watched as the large dino crab tumbled out, pinched its claws at him, and scuttled away. It headed towards the stream, its silvery shell sparkling in the sunshine.

The stunned raptor stood up, shook itself, and looked around menacingly. Its tail feathers stiffened as it spotted the silvery crab scuttling past. The raptor lunged after the crab.

The crab darted this way and that, as the raptor turned, crouched, and sprang towards the crab.

Snap!

The raptor's teeth crunched together on thin air.

"The poor crab hasn't got a chance!" Tess yelled from the ledge above the cave.

But both Jamie and Tess stared in

amazement as the crab waved its pincers defiantly at the raptor, scuttled towards it, and pinched it on the back of its leg.

Ack! The raptor leapt back in surprise and pain.

"Go, crab, go!" the friends cheered, as the crab scuttled away from the raptor, towards the tumbling stream. They watched it plop into the water and sail like a boat downstream towards Misty Lagoon.

The velociraptor raced after the crab, dodging spouts of hot steam as one after another the geysers erupted all around it.

"The crab can take care of itself." Tess laughed. "That velociraptor has met its match!"

Jamie looked at his watch. "We better get back." Jamie yelled up to Tess.

"I can see Ginkgo Hill from up here," Tess called down. "We can go across the plains."

"Great!" Jamie grabbed the bucket and he and Wanna clambered up onto the rock ledge above the cave. As they climbed, the green top of Ginkgo Hill rose in the distance. "I'm glad we don't have to go back through the geysers."

Wanna greeted Tess with a wag of his tail, then strode off along the narrow path that led away from the cave. At the top, Jamie put down the bucket and shaded his eyes to look out across the gently rolling plains that lay between them and Ginkgo Hill. On the edge of the plains, a herd of small stocky dinosaurs with big bony neck frills and parrot-like beaks was grazing peacefully on the horsetail ferns.

Jamie rummaged in his backpack and took out the tablet. Its shiny case was dented with raptor tooth marks. He rubbed off a streak of dried raptor dribble and switched it on.

Immediately, a Dinosaur Club message popped up.

Hi Jamie and Tess! Are you in Dino World?" wrote Ana from Brazil.

"It still works," Jamie said. He snapped a photo of the dinosaurs and pressed send.

"In the Cretaceous," he typed, while Tess read over his shoulder. "Any idea what these are?"

75

Tess put the crab line in the bucket and picked it up. "It's a good sign they're grazing," she said. "They wouldn't be so relaxed if any carnivores were around."

Wanna bobbed his head as if in agreement, turned and set off towards Ginkgo Hill followed by Tess. Jamie crammed the tablet into his backpack and hurried after them.

"He knows all the paths around here," Tess said, as Wanna confidently led them past the herd of peaceful protoceratops and through the jumbles of rock and tangles of tree ferns that dotted the plains. They followed the little dinosaur across the stream and back up the hillside to the top of Ginkgo Hill.

Jamie checked his watch. "We should

make it in time to meet Grandad," he said, giving Wanna a pat on the head. "Bye, Wanna, see you next time. Sorry I accused you of stealing my sandwich."

Jamie picked a handful of ginkgo fruit and the little dinosaur grunked happily as he settled down by his nest and began to munch on the stinky fruit.

Tess looked at her watch. "We'll have to hurry," she announced. The two friends carefully placed their feet over the fresh dinosaur prints outside the rock face, and stepped backwards out of the bright sunshine of Dino World into the darkness of the smugglers' cave. They squeezed though the gap, dashed out of the cave, and burst out onto Smuggler's Point.

Beneath them the waves were swirling close to the rocks.

"The beach will be cut off any minute now," Tess panted. "It's almost high tide."

They sprinted down the path and
reached the beach just as the first gentle
waves lapped at the bottom of
the pathway.

"Just in time!" Jamie shouted, as they
splashed through the shallow water and
hurried to the other side of the cove.

"Ahoy there, me hearties!"
Commander Morgan greeted them with
a wave from the rocks.

"Are you ready for a crabbing adventure?"

"Just as long as there are no geysers or raptors," Tess whispered to Jamie as they scrambled up the rocks to join him.

Jamie grinned. "Ahoy there, Grandad," he called. "We're always ready for a new adventure!"

Dinosaur timeline

The Triassic
(250-200 million years ago)

The first period of the Mesozoic Era was the Triassic.
During the Triassic, there were very few plants, and
the Earth was hot and dry, like a desert. Most of the
dinosaurs that lived during the Triassic were small.

The Jurassic
(200-145 million years ago)

The second period of the Mesozoic Era was the Jurassic.
During the Jurassic, the Earth became cooler and wetter,
which caused lots of plants to grow. This created lots of
food for dinosaurs that helped them grow big and thrive.

The Cretaceous
(145-66 million years ago)

The third and final period of the Mesozoic Era was the
Cretaceous. During the Cretaceous, dinosaurs were at
their peak and dominated the Earth, but at the end
most of them suddenly became extinct.

Dinosaurs existed during a time on Earth known as the Mesozoic Era. It lasted for more than 180 million years, and was split into three different periods: the Triassic, Jurassic, and the Cretaceous.

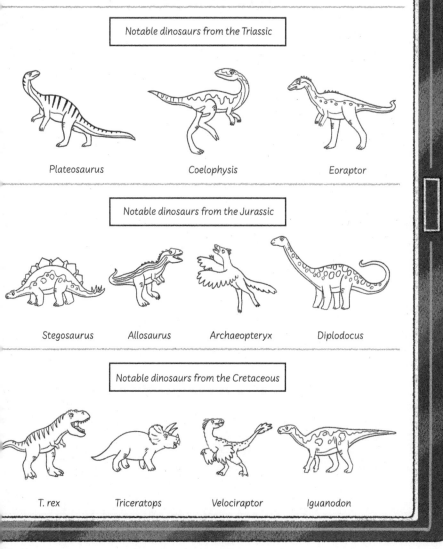

Notable dinosaurs from the Triassic

Plateosaurus   Coelophysis   Eoraptor

Notable dinosaurs from the Jurassic

Stegosaurus   Allosaurus   Archaeopteryx   Diplodocus

Notable dinosaurs from the Cretaceous

T. rex   Triceratops   Velociraptor   Iguanodon

FAR AWAY MOUNTAINS

CRASHING
ROCK
FALLS

FANG
ROCK

GREAT PLAINS

GINKGO
HILL

DINO DATA

This feathered predator may have been small, but it was fast, vicious, and may have worked as a team to hunt its prey.

Feathers

Name: Velociraptor
Pronounciation: vel-OSS-ee-RAP-tor
Period: Cretaceous
Size: 2m (6½ ft) long
Habitat: Scrubland and deserts
Diet: Meat

FACT

"Velociraptor" means "speedy thief".

FACT

Velociraptor had one extra long claw on each foot.

Sharp claws

DINO DATA

This little dinosaur was about the size of a large pig. Its large head frill made up about one fifth of its body size.

Armoured frill ———

Beak

Name: Protoceratops

Pronounciation: PRO-toe-SERRA-tops

Period: Cretaceous

Size: 2m (6½ ft) long

Habitat: Deserts

Diet: Plants

FACT

To stay safe from predators, protoceratops travelled in herds.

FACT

Protoceratops belonged to a group of dinosaurs called Ceratopsians, which also included Triceratops.

DINO DATA

Also known as T.rex, Tyrannosaurus was the most powerful and dangerous land predator of all time. It is sometimes called "King of the Dinosaurs".

Long tail for balancing

Powerful legs

Name: Tyrannosaurus
Pronunciation: tie-RAN-oh-SORE-us
Period: Cretaceous
Size: 12m (39ft) long
Habitat: Forests and swamps
Diet: Meat

Huge head

Sharp teeth

Small arms

FACT

The name Tyrannosaurus
means "tyrant lizard".

QUIZ

1   What bait do Jamie and Tess put on the crab lines?

2   True or false: A velociraptor's body was covered in feathers.

3   What period did Jamie and Tess travel to?

4   True or false: Geysers are caused by melted rock deep within the Earth.

5   What object does the velociraptor steal?

6   True or false: Velociraptor is
      a plant-eater.

CHECK YOUR ANSWERS on page 95

GLOSSARY

AMMONITE
A type of sea creature that lived during the time of the dinosaurs

CARNIVORE
An animal that only eats meat

CRETACEOUS
The third period of the time dinosaurs existed (145-65 million years ago)

DINOSAUR
A group of ancient reptiles that lived millions of years ago

FOSSIL
Remains of a living thing that have become preserved over time

GINKGO
A type of tree that dates back millions of years

HERBIVORE
An animal that only eats plant matter

PALAEONTOLOGIST
A scientist who studies dinosaurs and other fossils

PTEROSAUR
Ancient flying reptiles that existed at the same time as dinosaurs

PREDATOR
An animal that hunts other animals for food

QUIZ ANSWERS
1. Bacon
2. True
3. The Cretaceous
4. True
5. Jamie's tablet
6. False

Text for DK by Working Partners Ltd
9 Kingsway, London WC2B 6XF
With special thanks to Jane Clarke

For Sara O'Connor and everyone at Working Partners

Design by Collaborate Ltd
Illustrator Louise Forshaw
Consultant Dougal Dixon

Acquisitions Editor James Mitchem
Senior Designer and Jacket Designer Elle Ward
Publishing Coordinator Issy Walsh
Production Editor Abi Maxwell
Production Controller Isabell Schart
Publishing Director Sarah Larter

First published in Great Britain in 2022 by
Dorling Kindersley Limited
One Embassy Gardens, 8 Viaduct Gardens,
London, SW11 7AY

Text copyright © Working Partners Ltd 2008
Copyright in the layouts, design, and illustrations
of the Work shall be vested in the Publishers.
A Penguin Random House Company
10 9 8 7 6 5 4 3 2 1
001-328745-Dec/2022

All rights reserved.
No part of this publication may be reproduced, stored
in or introduced into a retrieval system, or transmitted,
in any form, or by any means (electronic, mechanical, photocopying,
recording, or otherwise), without the
prior written permission of the copyright owner.

A CIP catalogue record for this book
is available from the British Library.
ISBN: 978-0-2415-5917-8

Printed and bound in Great Britain by
Clays Ltd, Elcograf S.p.A.

www.dk.com
For the curious

This book was made with Forest Stewardship Council ™
certified paper – one small step in DK's commitment
to a sustainable future. For more information go to
www.dk.com/our-green-pledge